TRY NOT TO LAUGH

What do you call a dinosaur
that is sleeping?

A dino-snore!

What is fast, loud and crunchy?

A rocket chip!

Why did the teddy bear say no
to dessert?

Because she was stuffed.

What has ears but cannot hear?

A cornfield.

What did the left eye
say to the right eye?

Between us, something smells!

What do you get when you cross
a vampire and a snowman?

Frost bite!

When you look for
something, why is it always
in the last place you look?

Because when you find it, you stop looking.

Why did the student
eat his homework?

Because the teacher told him it
was a piece of cake!

What is brown, hairy
and wears sunglasses?

A coconut on vacation.

How do you stop
an astronaut's baby from crying?

You rocket!

What do you call a droid that
takes the long way around?

R2 detour.

How does a vampire start a letter?

Tomb it may concern...

When does a joke become
a "dad" joke?

When the punchline is a parent.

What is a witch's favorite
subject in school?

Spelling!

Why was 6 afraid of 7?

Because 7, 8, 9

What do you call
a duck that gets all A's?

A wise quacker.

What did the limestone
say to the geologist?

Don't take me for granite!

How do you make a lemon drop?

Just let it fall.

Why does a seagull fly over the sea?

Because if it flew over the bay,
it would be a baygull.

What kind of water cannot freeze?

Hot water.

What kind of tree fits in your hand?

A palm tree!

Why did the cookie
go to the hospital?

Because he felt crummy.

Why was the baby strawberry
crying?

Because her parents were in a jam.

What did the little corn
say to the mama corn?

Where is pop corn?

What is worse than
raining cats and dogs?

Hailing taxis!

How much does it cost
a pirate to get his ears pierced?

About a buck an ear.

Where would you find an elephant?

The same place you lost her!

How do you talk to a giant?

Use big words!

What animal is always
at a baseball game?

A bat.

What falls in winter
but never gets hurt?

Snow!

What do you call
a ghost's true love?

His ghoul-friend.

What building in New York
has the most stories?

The public library!

What did one volcano
say to the other?

I lava you!

How do we know that
the ocean is friendly?

It waves!

What is a tornado's
favorite game to play?

Twister!

How does the moon cut his hair?

Eclipse it.

How do you get
a squirrel to like you?

Act like a nut!

What do you call two birds in love?

Tweethearts!

How does a scientist freshen
her breath?

With experi-mints!

How are false teeth like stars?

They come out at night!

How can you tell a vampire has a cold?

She starts coffin.

What's worse than finding a worm in your apple?

Finding half a worm.

What is a computer's favorite snack?

Computer chips!!
—reader Rebecca K.

Why don't elephants chew gum?

They do, just not in public.

What was the first animal in space?

The cow that jumped over the moon

What did the banana
say to the dog?

Nothing. Bananas can't talk.

What time is it when
the clock strikes 13?

Time to get a new clock.

How does a cucumber become
a pickle?

It goes through a jarring experience.

What do you call a boomerang
that won't come back?

A stick.

Why did the dinosaur cross
the road?

Because the chicken wasn't born yet.

What do you think of that
new diner on the moon?

Food was good, but there really
wasn't much atmosphere.

Why can't Elsa have a balloon?

Because she will let it go.

How do you make an octopus laugh?

With ten-tickles!

How do you make a tissue dance?

You put a little boogie in it.

What's green and can fly?

Super Pickle!

What did the nose say to the finger?

Quit picking on me!

What musical instrument is found
in the bathroom?

A tuba toothpaste.

Why did the kid bring a ladder to school?

Because she wanted to go to high school.

What is a vampire's favorite fruit?

A blood orange.

What do elves learn in school?

The elf-abet.

What do you call a dog magician?

A labracadabrador.

Where do pencils go on vacation?

Pencil-vania.

Why couldn't the pony sing a lullaby?

She was a little horse.

Why didn't the skeleton go to the dance?

He had no body to dance with.

What gets wetter the more it dries?

A towel.

What do you call two bananas?

Slippers.

And speaking of bananas...

Why did the banana go
to the doctor?

Because it wasn't peeling well.

What do you call a fake noodle?

An impasta.

What stays in the corner yet can
travel all over the world?

A stamp.

How do you fix a cracked pumpkin?

With a pumpkin patch.

What kind of award did the dentist receive?

A little plaque.

What do you call a funny mountain?

Hill-arious.

Why are ghosts bad liars?

Because you can see right
through them.

Why do bees have sticky hair?

Because they use a honeycomb.

What did the big flower
say to the little flower?

Hi, bud!

What part of your body can cause the end of the world?

Your apoco-lips

What did the astronaut say when he crashed into the moon?

"I Apollo-gize."

Why didn't the orange win the race?

It ran out of juice.

What dinosaur had
the best vocabulary?

The thesaurus.

Why aren't dogs good dancers?

They have two left feet.

What did the wolf say when
it stubbed its toe?

Owwwww-ch!

Why did Johnny throw the clock out of the window?

Because he wanted to see time fly.

What did one toilet say to the other?

You look flushed.

Why did the man put his money in the freezer?

He wanted cold hard cash!

Why couldn't the astronaut book a hotel on the moon?

Because it was full.

How do pickles enjoy a day out?

They relish it.

What do you call an old snowman?

Water.

What's a pirate's favorite letter?

Arrrrrrrrrr

What do you get when you
cross an elephant with a fish?

Swimming trunks.

How do you throw a party in space?

You planet.

What did zero say to eight?

Nice belt!

What do you call a sleeping bull?

A bulldozer!

What happened when
the skunk was on trial?

The judge declared, "Odor in the court,
odor in the court!"

Why did the tomato blush?

It saw the salad dressing.

What do you call a fish without an eye?

A fsh.

What's the difference between roast beef and pea soup?

Anyone can roast beef.

What do you get when
you cross a centipede
with a parrot?

A walkie talkie

Why are robots never afraid?

They have nerves of steel.

Why did the cabbage win the race?

Because it was a-head

What does an evil hen lay?

Deviled eggs

What does a book do in the winter?

Puts on a jacket

What sound do you hear when
a cow breaks the sound barrier?

Cowboom!

What kind of haircuts
to bees get?

Buzzzzzcuts

What do you get if you cross
a pie and a snake?

A pie-thon

What do you do if you
get peanut butter on your doorknob?

Use a door jam

Why didn't the robot
finish his breakfast?

Because the orange juice told him to concentrate.

Why can't you play hockey with pigs?

They always hog the puck.

Why do porcupines
always win the game?

They have the most points

Where do elephants
pack their clothes?

In their trunks!

What does bread do on vacation?

Loaf around

Why was the broom running late?

It over-swept

What part of the fish weighs the most?

The scales

What do ghosts like to eat in the summer?

I Scream

Why did the teacher wear sunglasses to school?

Because her students were so bright

Where do sheep go on vacation?

The Baaa-hamas

What does every birthday end with?

The letter Y

What did the paper say
to the pencil?

Write on!

Why do birds fly?

It's faster than walking

Why did Superman flush the toilet?

Because it was his doody

Why did the pillow cross the road?

It was picking up the chicken's feathers

Can February March?

No, but April May

What time do ducks wake up?

At the quack of dawn

Why did the giraffes get bad grades?

She had her head in the clouds

What did the flower say after
it told a joke?

I was just pollen your leg

What did the traffic light
say to the truck?

Don't look, I'm changing

What does a cloud wear?

Thunderwear

Why didn't the koala bear get the job?

They said she was over-koala-fied

Who was that owl who did all the tricks?

Who-dini

What kind of vegetable is angry?

A steamed carrot!

How does the moon
stay up in the sky?

Moonbeams

Why isn't there a clock
in the library?

Because it tocks too much

Why do you never see elephants
hiding in trees?

Because they're so good at it!

What day of the week
are most twins born on?

Twos-day!

Would February March?

No, but April May

What do you call bears with
no ears?

B

What kind of tree fits in your hand?

A palm tree!

Where do rocks like to sleep?

Bedrock!

How do you pay for parking in space?

A parking meteor

What do you call
two giraffes colliding?

A giraffe-ic jam

What animal is always
at a baseball game?

A bat

What did the reporter say
to the ice cream?

"What's the scoop?"

How do you get fired
from a coin-mint?

You stop making cents

What do you call a fly with
no wings?

A walk

What did the lunchbox say
to the banana?

You really have appeal

What did the mouse
say to the keyboard?

You're my type!

What did the science book
say to the math book?

Wow, you've got problems

How do squids get to school?

They take an octobus

Where do mermaids look for jobs?

The kelp-wanted section

Why is there a gate around cemeteries?

Because people are dying to get in

What is a scarecrow's favorite fruit?

A strawberry

How does a hurricane see?

With one eye

How do they answer
the phone at the paint store?

Yellow!

Why do scissors always win a race?

Because they take a shortcut!

What do you call two monkeys
that share an Amazon account?

Primemates!

What snack should you make for
the Snowman Holiday Party?

Ice Krispy Treats

What do you call
a nun who sleepwalks?

A roamin' Catholic

TRY NOT TO LAUGH